The Clue in the Castle

A WOODLAND MYSTERY

By Irene Schultz

To Enid Hennesey and Marion Russell, two great teachers

The Clue in the Castle

Cover and cameo illustrations by Taylor Bruce
Interior illustrations by Meredith Yasui, Tom Boatman, and Charles Solway
Map illustration by Alicia Kramer

Woodland Mysteries™

The Woodland Mysteries were created by the Wright Group development team.

The Wright Group
19201 120th Avenue NE
Bothell, WA 98011

Printed in the United States of America

10 9 8 7 6 5 4 3

ISBN: 0-7802-7237-4

What family solves mysteries...has adventures all over the world...and loves oatmeal cookies?

It's the Woodlanders!

Sammy Westburg (10 years old)
His sister Kathy Westburg (13)
His brother Bill Westburg (14)
His best friend Dave Briggs (16)
His best grown-up friend Mrs. Tandy
And Mop, their little dog!

The children all lost their parents, but with Mrs. Tandy have made their own family.

Why are they called the Woodlanders? Because they live in a big house in the Bluff Lake woods. On Woodland Street!

Together they find fun, mystery, and adventure. What are they up to now?

Read on!

Meet the Woodlanders!

Sammy Westburg
Sammy is a ten-year-old wonder! He's big for his fifth-grade class, and big-mouthed, too. He has wild hair and makes awful spider faces. Even so, you can't help liking him.

Bill Westburg
Bill, fourteen, is friendly and strong, and only one inch taller than his brother Sammy. He loves Sammy, but pokes him to make him be quiet! He's in junior high.

Kathy Westburg
Kathy, thirteen, is small, shy, and smart. She wants to be a doctor someday! She loves to be with Dave, and her brothers kid her about it. She's in junior high, too.

Dave Briggs

Dave, sixteen, is tall and blond. He can't walk, so he uses a wheelchair and drives a special car. He likes coaching high-school sports, solving mysteries, and reading. And Kathy!

Mrs. Tandy

Sometimes the kids call her Mrs. T. She's Becky Tandy, their tall, thin, caring friend. She's always ready for a new adventure, and for making cookies!

Mop

Mop is the family's little tan dog. Sometimes they have to leave him behind with friends. But he'd much rather be running after Sammy.

Table of Contents

Chapter 1: Off to England

"The mail's here!" called thirteen-year-old Kathy Westburg.

Her two brothers, ten-year-old Sammy and fourteen-year-old Bill, raced across the grass.

Bill got to the mail truck first.

Sammy tried to get the letters, but the driver handed them to Bill instead.

She said, "You're the winner, Bill!"

Then she called to Mrs. Tandy, "The Woodlanders all got mail today, but yours is the best, Becky! It's from England!"

Dave Briggs, sixteen, rolled his wheel chair over to Mrs. Tandy on the porch.

The others gathered around her.

Sammy said, "What did you get? Can we see?"

Bill poked him. He said, "It's HERS! She will show us if she feels like it."

Sammy said, "Don't poke me!" He threw a handful of grass on Bill's head.

Mrs. Tandy looked over her letter.

She said, "My goodness, listen to this! You know how we've been talking about taking a trip when school is out? Maybe to Texas or Mexico?"

Sammy said, "What's that got to do with your letter?"

Mrs. Tandy said, "This! How would you like to go to England for the summer?"

Kathy shouted, "ENGLAND! I'd love to go there. Why? What's in the letter?"

Mrs. Tandy said, "My mother's aunt died. I never met her, but we've been writing to each other for years.

"This letter says she left me some money and a cottage in England. It's in a town called Martin-on-the-River."

Sammy yelled, "Yipee! Let's go!" He did a backward roll. His feet landed on Bill's chest.

Bill jumped up and took hold of Sammy's feet. He pulled him like a wagon, right into the woods.

Bill came back to the porch and said, "NOW we can make plans."

Kathy asked, "When can we go?"

Mrs. Tandy said, "The last day of school is June 10. We could get our passports by then."

Dave said, "It'll take a day to get the house in shape and a day to pack. How about leaving on the third day after school's out?"

Bill said, "All right! I can hardly wait."

Kathy said, "Just a minute ... what will we do with Mop?"

At the sound of his name, their shaggy tan dog opened one eye and lifted his head.

Then he put it down on his paw and went back to sleep in the sun.

Mrs. Tandy said, "I'd hate to put him in a dog kennel for the whole summer.

I bet the Strongs would take care of him for us."

Dave said, "Well, then I'll call about our plane tickets!"

Sammy, back from the woods, pulled a leaf out of his hair.

He said, "Bill and I can get the suitcases down from the garage shelf. In fact, let's do it right now!"

He pulled Bill by the hand. His older brother smiled and went along.

Dave said, "I get the feeling this trip is going to be a big adventure."

Mrs. Tandy said, "Sure it is ... but why do you think so?"

Dave said, "Well, we are going to a country we've never gone to before."

Kathy added, "To stay in a house we've never seen."

Mrs. Tandy said, "Which belonged to a great aunt I never met."

Bill and Sammy put the bags onto the porch.

Bill said, "Let's finish up our work in the yard. I can trim out some more dead branches in the woods."

Everybody got back to their weeding, planting, and raking.

No one talked.

But everyone was thinking, "England! England! ENGLAND!"

Chapter 2: English Friends

School finally got out for the summer.

Three days later, the Woodlanders stood in the dining room ... with suit-cases everywhere.

Kathy cried, "This looks like a suitcase store!"

Bill said, "The taxi's here. Let's get going."

They put everything into the taxi van waiting outside.

As they got in, Sammy said in a scary voice, "I counted the bags. THIRTEEN! Bad luck!"

Bill said, "The only bad-luck part is that we have to carry all this stuff."

Dave said, "You don't really believe the number thirteen is bad luck, do you, Sammy? You just like to scare yourself."

Sammy said, "Well, that's what the kids say all the time at school."

Mrs. Tandy said, "Then we will try to be extra careful on this trip, Sammy."

They shut the doors and the van drove away.

At the airport they went to their gate

and sat down to wait.

Across from them sat a couple with a little boy about two years old.

The little boy kept looking at Dave in his wheelchair. He smiled and made a face.

Then he got out of his seat and walked up to Dave. The next minute he had climbed into Dave's lap!

Dave smiled and hugged him.

When the mother saw where her son was, she called, "Bunny, come here!"

They could tell she was English from the way she spoke.

She ran over to Dave. She said, "I'm so sorry he bothered you." She reached to take him back.

But Dave said, "He can stay here with me. He's no trouble at all. So his name is really Bunny?"

She said, "It's really Benny. Ben, like his father's. I'm Mrs. Hunter. Liz Hunter. You're sure you don't mind putting up with Bunny here?"

Dave said, "Of course not!" and Bunny hugged him.

Mrs. Hunter laughed and went back to her seat.

Her husband nodded hello to the Woodlanders. He asked, "Are you going to stay in London for a while?"

The Woodlanders could tell he was from England, too.

Sammy answered, "Just for a couple of days to hear a will being read, and to look around."

Bill said, "Then we are going to the country."

Mrs. Tandy asked the couple, "Where are you from?"

Mrs. Hunter said, "We live in London."

By then Bunny had grabbed Dave's nose. He was standing on Dave's lap and messing up his hair.

Dave hugged him again, and Bunny gave him a big wet kiss on his eyebrow.

Kathy said, "Dave, it looks to me like Bunny adopted you. I don't think he's ever going to let you go."

Dave laughed. "Well, he has to let me go for a little while. I have to go check us in."

He handed Bunny back to Mrs. Hunter and wheeled off to the counter.

She put Bunny on the seat next to her. He dropped off to sleep right away.

She said, "I think Ben and I need a nap, too."

Sammy said, "Hey, guys. Let's go get some food. We take off at noon and won't eat until later. I'm STARVED!"

They all walked off to get some sand-wiches.

Dave was just leaving the check-in counter when they got back.

Bill handed him a sandwich. He said, "Here. You have just about ten minutes to eat it!"

They went back to their seats.

Mr. and Mrs. Hunter were waking up from their naps. Mr. Hunter looked all around.

He gasped, "Bunny is gone! He must

have run off while we were sleeping!"

Mrs. Hunter cried, "Oh, no! Where can he be?"

Kathy said, "Don't worry. We can help you find him."

Dave said, "Spread out, guys!"

One minute before boarding time they met back at their gate. No Bunny.

But just then Bill came running down the hall with Bunny on his back.

He called, "Hey, stop choking me, Bunny!"

Bunny yelled, "Gid-ee-up, horsy!"

Mrs. Hunter said, "Oh, thank you, thank you." She peeled Bunny off of Bill's back. She was so glad to see him, she started to cry.

Bunny kissed her on the cheek. Then he wiggled down out of her arms.

He said, "I want my horsy." He climbed into Bill's arms and onto his back again.

Mr. Hunter said, "Good job, Bill. How did you ever find him?"

Bill said, "It wasn't too hard. I've kept track of Sammy for years now. So I just kept thinking of where Sammy would go.

"First I looked around the candy machine.

"And then I looked around the potato-chip machine.

"Then the popcorn cart.

"And then I had a brainstorm. I went right to the snack bar.

"There was Bunny, sitting on the floor, chewing on part of a hot dog someone had dropped."

Sammy made a face and said, "Yuck!"

Mrs. Hunter said, "Good heavens. I wonder how many feet stepped on it before he ate it ..."

Mr. Hunter said, "His nickname shouldn't be Bunny. Maybe Piggy would be more like it."

He took Bunny in his arms and gave him a huge hug.

"Flight one-thirteen, boarding for London," said a voice on a loudspeaker.

Mr. Hunter said, "I won't forget your kindness. But now we'd all better get aboard."

Chapter 3: Crossing the Atlantic

Soon the Woodlanders were fastening their seat belts for take-off.

The engines whined.

The plane moved to the runway.

Bill said, "Good-bye, America! England here we come!"

Sammy said, "Rotten rats! Get this! Thirteen bags. Flight number one-thirteen!

"And today is Friday the thirteenth! It says so here on my ticket. No WONDER Bunny got lost. It IS a bad-luck day!"

Bill said, "But we found him, right? So it's a GOOD-luck day."

Sammy said, "Hey, I can't wait to see Mrs. Tandy learning to drive on the left side of the road.

"That's what you have to do in England, you know. I bet it's HARD! She's going to be SCARED!"

Bill said, "Not with you telling her how to do it, Oh Great One."

Sammy stuck his tongue out at Bill so far it hurt. He took out a deck of cards and said, "Come on. I'll teach you how to lose at rummy, Motor Mouth."

Just then Mrs. Hunter walked up to them. She thanked Bill again for finding Bunny, and wrote down each of their names.

She said, "I'll come back later to say hello!"

Sammy whispered, "Why did she take down our names?"

Bill whispered back, "I have no idea."

In a little while they ate lunch. It was chicken and gravy and noodles and green beans and rolls and butter and salad and cake and orange juice and milk.

Sammy said, "I think I'll just spend the whole summer flying back and forth across the Atlantic Ocean, and eating great food."

Dinner was even better.

They fell asleep after the movie, when

the lights were turned low. They slept for hours.

All of a sudden Sammy woke up. He said, "Hey! Something's hurting my ears."

Mrs. Tandy said, "Open your mouth and yawn a little. Or swallow, and they'll feel better."

Dave added, "Wow! We must be going down already! Your ears feel funny because of the change in air pressure, Sammy."

In twenty minutes they landed. Before they had their bags out from under the seats, the Hunters walked by. Mr. Hunter handed them a note:

Dear Becky, Dave, Bill, Kathy and Sammy,

Liz and I would be happy to have you come to our house for dinner. I'm sure Bunny would be happy too. Are you tough enough to stand him? Please phone us later today when you've had a rest.

With thanks, Ben and Liz Hunter

479-6720

A phone number was written below. They all thought it would be fun.

Mrs. Tandy said, "Then we WILL phone them, and we will go! But now, let's get off this plane and on to our hotel!"

They piled all their bags onto two carts. Then they waited for the hotel bus.

At last, at 2:00 in the morning, they made it to their hotel.

There was one room for the three boys, and one for Mrs. Tandy and Kathy.

They were so tired, they almost fell into bed.

Sammy said, "Sleep well, you guys. We have to be in good shape for later. Dinner with good old pesty Bunny, you know."

Bill said, "OK. Good-night, good old pesty Sammy."

With his last bit of strength, Sammy threw his pillow at Bill's bed. It landed on Dave's head by mistake.

Dave said, "We've come all the way

across the Atlantic Ocean to another country. But why does it seem just like home?"

Chapter 4: Dinner at the Hunters'

At 11:00 in the morning, Bill felt something on his nose.

Years of living with Sammy made him know Sammy was awake ... and up to no good.

When Bill opened his eyes he saw a ball of soft paper hanging on a string. Sammy was bouncing it on his nose.

Bill grabbed it and stuffed it under his pillow ... to use on Sammy's nose another morning.

The boys dressed and knocked on the door that joined their room to the next.

In came Kathy, ready to go.

Mrs. Tandy was talking on the phone. They heard her say, "Sounds wonderful, Liz. Seven o'clock tonight."

Dave said, "Perfect! Now, let's eat and take a look at London."

They had tea, toast, runny eggs, and sausage at the hotel.

Then they started walking around the city. First they stopped at Mrs. Tandy's lawyer's office. As they left, he gave her the keys for her new cottage.

Then they looked at about a hundred

shop windows.

They went to the national museum.

By 7:00 that night, the tired, hungry Woodlanders stood outside a huge home.

A big stairway led up to the Hunters' front door.

Sammy said, "Good grief! Look at all those steps! I've walked my feet off!

"You'll have to drag me the rest of the way."

But somehow he and Bill made it up the long front stairs with Dave in his wheelchair.

They rang the bell.

Mr. Hunter didn't answer the door.

Or Mrs. Hunter.

The door was opened by a man nearly seven feet tall ... as tall as the biggest basketball star they had ever seen.

He was dressed in a white shirt and a black suit.

He said, "Come in, young sirs, madam, and miss. The Hunters are expecting you."

Sammy said, "HOLY CATS!"

Then he walked all around the man for a better look. He said, "You're a butler, I bet! I've seen guys like you on TV. You look great!"

Bill and Kathy poked him.

Sammy said, "Stop poking me! He's the best and biggest butler I've ever seen!"

The butler tried to hide his smile.
He said, "Thank you, sir. My name is

Roger. Do let me hang up your coats."

Then he took them to the living room. It was huge, too.

Sammy said, "Wow! You could skateboard in here!"

Just then Bunny ran into the room and made a dive for Dave's lap. Then the Hunters came in.

Mrs. Hunter said, "We are so glad to see you. You must be hungry and tired. Let's talk over dinner."

They went into the dining room.

Mrs. Tandy told them about her great aunt's house. She added, "It's in a town called Martin-on-the-River."

Mrs. Hunter dropped her fork in surprise. "I can't believe it! Why, we are going to be there in one week ourselves!"

Mr. Hunter said, "You see, Liz and I work as archeologists for the national museum.

"I direct the digging. She's in charge of deciding just what we have un-covered."

Sammy said, "What's an AR-key-ahl-uh-jist?"

Mrs. Hunter said, "A person who studies signs of past human life ... like old bones or pieces of pottery."

Sammy said, "You get to look at old bones! Wow, I think THAT'S what I'm going to be when I grow up! An archeologist!"

Mr. Hunter smiled and went on. "We are following up on an old story of hidden treasure.

"People believe there was a Roman villa somewhere around Martin-on-the-River, about sixteen hundred years ago.

"And a fortune in gold is said to be tucked away there."

Sammy said, "YOU'RE KIDDING!

GOLD? In a VILLA? But ... what's a villa?"

Mr. Hunter said, "An old Roman house, and the buildings for running a big farm. It probably had hot baths and beautiful tile pictures.

"The man who owned the villa was in charge of all the gold for the Roman troops in England.

"That's how the story goes, anyway. But who knows if it's true.

"We've never found a thing there from Roman days, except the roads themselves. Not even a coin! We don't know where to dig for the ruins."

Mrs. Hunter said, "This year we want to start as many digs outside of town as the museum can afford.

"It's become very important that we try to find the villa as soon as we can."

Kathy said, "Hunter is a great name

for you. You both hunt for old things."

Sammy said, "How come you live in such a big fancy house if you just work for a museum?"

Bill and Kathy both poked him again, hard.

Sammy made his poison-spider face at them. He said, "I SAID, quit poking me all the time!"

Both the Hunters laughed.

Mr. Hunter said, "The museum lets us

use this house between digs. The butler and the house are part of our pay."

Sammy asked, "Does the museum pay for a cook to make this yummy food?" He pointed to the small plate in front of him. He was just chewing the last bite from it.

Mrs. Hunter said, "Oh, no. You can buy what you just ate in any English food shop. It IS good, isn't it? I've always so enjoyed jellied eel."

Sammy said, "EEL! Those big shiny things that are always grabbing divers in the under-sea movies?"

Mr. Hunter said, "Right. Good, aren't they!" He took a huge bite.

Sammy swallowed the rest of his eel with a big gulp.

After dinner Mrs. Hunter wrote something on a piece of paper. She gave it to Kathy.

She said, "Here's where we will be staying in Martin-on-the-River. Let's get in touch with each other next week."

Mr. Hunter said, "Until then, there's a place I think you'd like to see. It's right near where you'll be.

"It's mostly just an old ruined castle. It burned down over a hundred years ago. But it's still beautiful.

"My family owns it. And there's one building left that will knock your socks off! I know. I played in it when I was a little lad."

He wrote down, "Heart Castle, five miles north-east of Martin-on-the-River."

Dave asked, "What's the building like?"

Mr. Hunter said, "It's a fat, round tower about forty feet tall. It's strong and has a good roof. My grandfather kept it in good shape as a playhouse for us."

Mrs. Hunter said, "But there are no floors in it."

Mr. Hunter added, "Yet there are hundreds of homes in it."

Bill said, "Aw, come on. What do you mean? Hundreds? In just one tower?"

Mr. Hunter said, "Yes, sir."

Bill said, "You're joking."

Mrs. Hunter said, "It's true! When we see you next, you tell us if you can figure out why."

The Woodlanders said their thanks and good-nights. They went back to the hotel.

Sammy said, "Well, tonight you guys HAVE to sleep well. Because tomorrow? We find Mrs. Tandy's new house AND the mystery tower!"

Chapter 5: The Ghostly Tower

The next day, they headed straight for Martin-on-the-River.

Mrs. Tandy was driving their red rental car.

For the hundredth time Sammy said, "Stay on the left side of the road."

They had given him the job of saying that every few minutes ... just in case Mrs. Tandy forgot.

Bill told Sammy, "After all, you're the one who likes to talk the most. It's the perfect job for you."

Dave said, "It's a good thing this car is so big. Thirteen suitcases WOULD have been bad luck in a little car. Even in two little cars."

Sammy said, "Stay on the left side of the road."

Kathy said, "We must be close, Mrs. T. We've been on the road for four hours."

Mrs. Tandy said, "The clerk at the hotel said it would take two hours, but I've been driving very slowly."

Dave said, "Look! That sign says HEART CASTLE: FIVE MILES, and this one

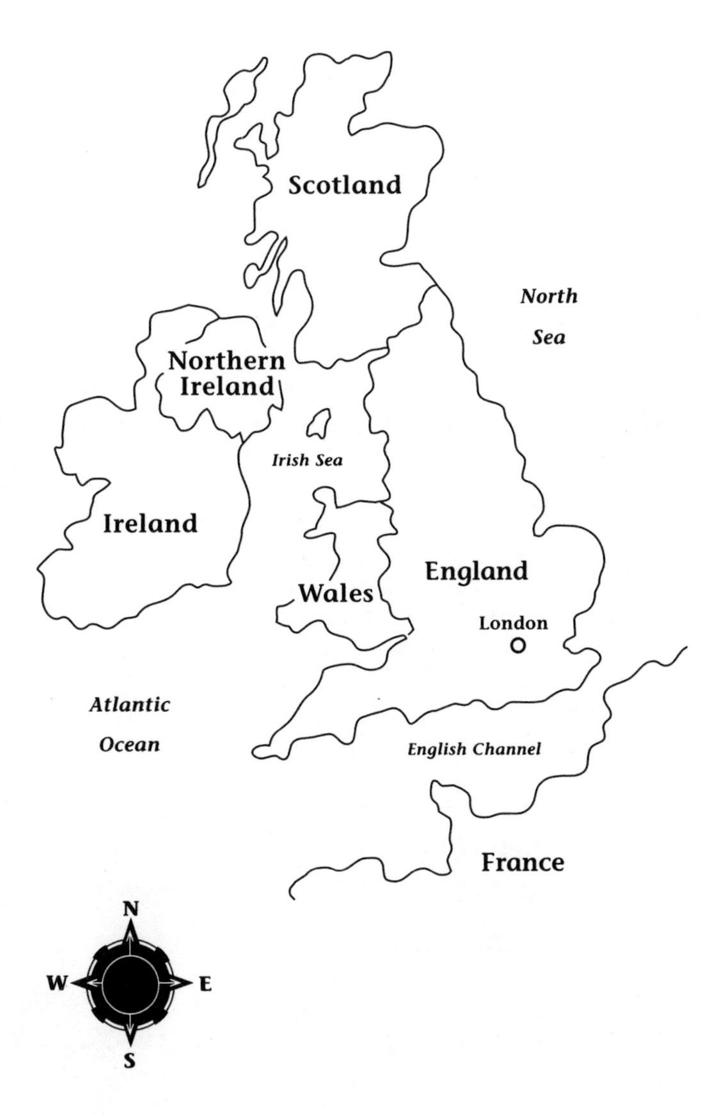
Scotland
North
Sea
Northern
Ireland
Irish Sea
Ireland
England
Wales
London
Atlantic
Ocean
English Channel
France
N
W
E
S

says MARTIN-ON-THE-RIVER. We must be at the edge of our new town!"

Sammy said, "Stay on the left side of the road."

Kathy said, "Look! Here's the street we want! Clover Road. Turn here, Mrs. T.!"

Sammy said, "Stay on the left side of the road."

And there it was.

Mrs. Tandy's English home.

1010 Clover Road.

Sammy said, "Man! It's sort of big!"

They went inside.

Sammy cried, "Will you look at this!"

He ran from room to room. He said, "A living room! A dining room! A kitchen! A bathroom! Even a huge bedroom on the first floor. Perfect for us three boys!"

Then he ran up the stairs. He said,

"There are three more bedrooms up here!"

The house was beautiful, with shining wood floors, clean white walls, and fine paintings.

Dave said, "Mrs. Tandy, look at this furniture. It looks like it's at least a hundred years old."

Mrs. Tandy said, "My great aunt's grandparents built this cottage. That was about a hundred and fifty years ago!"

They all took a quick look upstairs.

Kathy said, "Mrs. Tandy, I know you want to spend some time in your new house."

Sammy added, "And check out your new furniture."

Bill added, "And un-pack your bags. But do you think a little later today we could—"

Mrs. Tandy said, "First of all, quit calling it MY house! It's OUR house ... we are a family.

"And second, stop trying to be so nice to me! I'm dying to go to Heart Castle just as much as you. We can un-pack later. So let's go!"

Everybody cheered.

Bill and Sammy helped Dave out of the house.

Mrs. Tandy drove straight to Heart Castle. It was down a one-lane road with a wall of bushes on each side.

Sammy said, "Stay on the left side of the road."

Kathy said, "How can she? There's only one lane!"

Bill said, "You'd have to drive into an opening in the bushes if you saw another car."

Sammy said, "If you do have to pull off, stay on the left side of the road."

Suddenly some broken gray walls appeared over the far-off trees.

Dave cried, "There it is!"

Sammy said, "And there's the round tower! Wow! It's the fattest tower I've ever seen! Now stay on the left side of the road."

At last they were out of the car and racing over a stone path to the tower.

Sammy stood still in front of it. He said, "Hey, there's no door."

Dave said, "There must be one. Bill,

help me over the grass. We can go all around the tower."

Around the curving stone wall they went, pushing through chest-high weeds.

Kathy said, "Look at this!" She pointed to an opening in the wall, no taller than the weeds.

She pushed down the weeds in front of the doorway.

Sammy bent down and ran inside the tower.

He said, "I can't see! It's as black as a cave in here. Hey, what if there are spiders? I wouldn't be able to see them!" He sounded scared.

Dave bent down and wheeled himself inside. He said, "It's OK, Sammy. Your eyes will get used to the dark in a minute."

The others came in.

At first it was cool and black as night. At last their eyes got used to it.

Sammy yipped, "Wow! Look at all those cubby-holes."

Hundreds of holes the size of shoe boxes pitted the stone walls inside the tower.

Kathy said, "What IS this place?"

Bill said, "Remember? Mr. Hunter said there were hundreds of homes in this tower. Could these holes be the homes?"

Dave said, "That's it! The holes were

for bird nests. This must be the castle's dove house, where they used to raise doves for food."

Bill said, "Let's look around in the holes. Maybe we can find a hundred-year-old egg!"

Mrs. Tandy said, "Pew! I hope not!"

All of a sudden they heard a ghostly voice from the darkness above.

"Who-o-o is in my t-o-w-w-er?"

Chapter 6:
The Old Silver Box

A second later the ghostly voice began to giggle.

Kathy cried, "Sammy! What are you doing up there! You scared me to death!"

Sammy shouted down from near the roof, "These nest holes are great for climbing. Come on up!"

Bill said, "You come on down! You're twenty feet high! Get down here before you break a leg!"

Sammy said, "OK, I'm coming. But I'm going to find out what's in this one hole. When I put my hand in it, I felt something!"

He reached into the hole.

Then he shouted, "OK! I have it in my pocket. I'm coming down!"

He jumped the last few feet and said, "Come on outside. Let's see what it is."

They all headed out into the warm sunlight.

Sammy's hair was wild and full of spider webs.

Everyone crowded around him.

Bill said, "I'm sure glad you made it

down in one piece!" He picked a big spiderweb off Sammy's ear.

Sammy grinned. He pulled a small black metal box from his pocket. It had a beautiful design on the lid.

He held it out for them to see.

Dave said, "Hey, I saw some boxes like this in the national museum. I bet it's a silver snuff box. Silver turns black over time if you don't polish it.

"I bet it's more than a hundred years old."

Kathy said, "Be careful not to break it when you open it."

Sammy said, "Do you think someone put this box there that long ago? How come no kid ever found it before?"

Dave said, "How many kids do you think would climb halfway up a dove tower?"

Bill said, "Just two. Whoever put the

box there, and good old Sammy, that's how many."

Sammy waved the box back and forth. He said, "Something's shaking around inside it. Mrs. Tandy, you open it. You're good at things like this."

She said, "Goodness, I'll try."

She took the box and looked it over carefully. Then, very gently, she pushed in a small button and lifted the lid.

They all gasped when they saw what was inside. There was a folded piece of paper. And two old coins!

Sammy gulped. He said, "Wow! That's GOLD!"

Gently Mrs. Tandy pulled the paper out, leaving the coins in the box.

She said, "The fold must be very stiff if the paper's a hundred years old."

Then she opened the paper a little.

She read, "Wind-Born. Jonathan Hunter."

Bill said, "What else does it say?"
Mrs. Tandy said, "Nothing. That's all."

Dave said, "Wind-Born sounds like the name of a place."

Kathy said, "I wonder where it is. Maybe we can find it on a map."

Slowly Dave picked a coin out of the box. He said, "This has a man's head on it, and some words in Latin. It's an old Roman coin."

Kathy said, "There's a different man on this other coin. I bet these men were Roman emperors."

Bill said, "Listen, guys, we've got to get to a phone right away!"

Sammy asked, "Why?"

Bill said, "To call Mr. Hunter. Where there are Roman coins, there might be a Roman villa! We've got a clue, if we can find out where Wind-Born is."

Sammy cried, "That's just what I was going to say! LET'S GO! But stay on the left side of the road, Mrs. Tandy."

They drove to a restaurant to make the call to London.

When Mrs. Tandy got Mr. Hunter on the phone she said, "Hello. This is Becky Tandy. We have something very exciting to tell you!

"We ... Heart Castle ... Sammy ... gold coins ... Oh, my. I'm too excited to talk. I'll let Sammy do it."

Sammy got on. "Mr. Hunter! We found some coins! They were hidden high up in a nest hole, in the dove tower at Heart Castle.

"They're in an old silver box, with a note about a place called Wind-Born. The coins have writing on them. Dave says it's Latin."

Then Sammy said, "Ten-ten Clover Road. You won't! You do! It is! You are! You do! All right!"

Sammy hung up.

Kathy laughed and said, "What was all that about?"

Sammy said, "He's on his way!

"He knows where Wind-Born is!

"This is the first real clue he's ever had.

"So they're packing up tonight. They're coming with Bunny and Roger to meet us at the cottage at eight o'clock tomorrow morning.

"And here's the best part of all. He wants US to help with the search for the villa!"

Bill shouted, "Yipee!" and grabbed Mrs. Tandy. They did a wild dance right out on the sidewalk.

Then they rushed in to eat dinner at the restaurant.

The menu said fish and chips. But the chips turned out to be french fries!

Sammy said, "England sure is full of surprises!" and stuffed five french fries into his mouth at once.

After dinner they drove home.

Sammy said, "Stay on the left side of the road, Mrs. Tandy!"

The Woodlanders went right to bed so they would be ready for the next morning's treasure hunt.

Chapter 7: Where Do We Dig?

When the front doorbell of the cottage rang, the Woodlanders were already dressed.

Kathy ran to answer it.

There stood the Hunters, smiling from ear to ear.

Mrs. Tandy said, "Hello, there! Hi, Bunny! And where's Roger? Sammy said he was coming, too!"

Mrs. Hunter said, "Hi, everybody! Roger's running some errands right now, but he will be around later."

When Bunny saw Sammy he climbed right up his leg. Sammy held him in his arms and Bunny grabbed his nose. He gave it a twist.

"Ow!" shouted Sammy.

Bill said, "Now you know what it feels like to be an older brother ... it's a lifetime of having someone twist your nose."

Mrs. Hunter said, "Oh, I'm so sorry. Don't do that again, Bunny."

Sammy said, "He didn't hurt me. I'm tough. I'm used to my big mean brother trying to get me all the time."

■ ■ ■

As they talked, nobody noticed a man hiding under the side window. He moved closer to hear them better. He had secretly followed the Hunters from London!

■ ■ ■

Mr. Hunter said, "I can't tell you how excited I am about your phone call. I don't want to seem rude, but may I see the box right away?"

Sammy said, "It's right here!" and he opened it for the Hunters.

Mr. Hunter said, "I can hardly believe my eyes! These coins ARE Roman. They were made around four hundred A.D.

"That's just around the time the Roman troops all left this country. They had been at war here for many years.

"Many Romans were killed. Many villas were broken up. Finally, all the Romans here went back to Rome, Italy."

He read the note. "It's signed Jonathan Hunter. Why, I know who he was!

"He was just ten years old when he died in the fire at Heart Castle. He was the only one in the family who was killed."

Mrs. Tandy said, "Poor little boy. I wish he had lived. He must have been a lot like Sammy, to hide his coins way up there."

Dave said, "He must have meant to go back to Wind-Born to find more coins, but never made it."

Bill said to the Hunters, "Do you really know where Wind-Born is?"

Mrs. Hunter said, "Oh, yes. It's owned by Lord and Lady Frost. It's only a little way out of Martin-on-the-River.

"The Frosts are good friends of Ben's

father. They would be happy to help find the ruins. Why, they'd give that part of their farm to England, if we found the villa."

Mr. Hunter said, "But we have a big problem in front of us. Wind-Born Farm is huge."

Kathy said, "So the problem is where to start digging, right?"

He nodded.

Dave said, "Well, what are we waiting here for? Let's go take a look at Wind-Born, and get to work!"

Kathy said, "But Mrs. Tandy still hasn't had a chance to look over her ... I mean our ... new house!"

Mrs. Tandy said, "Plenty of time for that later. Let's go!"

▪ ▪ ▪

No one saw the man run away from the living-room window.

▪ ▪ ▪

Sammy said, "You take the box, Mr. Hunter. I think it would be safer with you.

"Besides, it belonged to your family. And I know you have to study the coins."

Mr. Hunter said, "Sammy, I can't thank you enough for this wonderful gift."

Then the Woodlanders and the Hunters drove off to Wind-Born.

Sammy was so excited, he even forgot to tell Mrs. Tandy to drive on the left side of the road.

Lord and Lady Frost hugged the Hunters and greeted the Woodlanders warmly.

Lord Frost got very excited when they told him why they had come.

He said, "That's the greatest surprise! Right here on Wind-Born Farm somewhere? We must find it! We shall find it, Ben!"

He hugged Ben Hunter again and said, "Let's walk over the farm. Maybe you'll get some idea of where to dig."

Then he took his thick walking stick from inside the door. He said to his wife, "Come, my dear. Let's show them around."

Lord Frost was a short man, red-faced and quite heavy. But he was a fast walker, and Lady Frost kept up with him every step.

Kathy pushed Dave along in his wheelchair, which wasn't easy!

Lord and Lady Frost took them over tree-covered hills.

They walked across little streams and around a lovely lake.

They passed through fields and under fruit trees.

They went up steps and over a stone wall.

At last Lord and Lady Frost stopped to let them rest. They were in a big field, covered with bushes.

Mrs. Tandy said, "How long have we walked? This is all so beautiful, I didn't realize how tired I was."

Lady Frost said, "You poor dear! We forgot you're not used to this. We tramp over the farm every day. We've tired you out.

"Now I know what we will do. You sit down right here in the rabbit field.

"The grass is dry and soft. This is the coolest spot on the farm."

Lord Frost said, "It's a perfect place to rest. I've often thought the house should have been built here."

Lady Frost said, "Well, I'm going to put some lunch things onto our golf cart. Then I'll drive back and we can have a nice picnic."

Sammy said, "I'll help you. Then you can count on me to drive the golf cart back.

"You'll have to show me how, but I know I can do it."

She laughed and put her hand into his. She said, "Let's go!"

After a while the others saw the cart coming back. Sammy was standing at the wheel. This time it was Sammy shouting, "Gid-ee-up, horsy!"

Bunny laughed and clapped his hands.

Lady Frost and Sammy had packed a huge basket of food. There was a big meat pie, orange juice, a large pot of tea, a bottle of milk for the tea, some berries, and some cookies.

Sammy said, "This meat pie doesn't have eel jelly in it, does it?" He looked at his piece as if it might bite him.

Everybody laughed.

They all sat on the grass and ate and talked.

But no one had any ideas about where to look for the old Roman villa.

Then, from the other end of the rabbit field, a man with a rake walked up to Lord Frost.

Lord Frost said, "Hello, James!" Then he said to the others, "This is James Hill. He farms my land."

Mr. Hill said, "Hello there! I came

over to tell you I'll be hunting rabbits tomorrow.

"This field is full of them, and they're eating every last bit of my garden. I've put up a big pen for them near my barn.

"Would you like to join in the job?"

Lord Frost said, "I'd be glad to, if my friends can come."

Kathy said, "So you'll keep the rabbits as pets, Mr. Hill?"

Mr. Hill laughed. "Pets, child? No, no. I do, however, make a fine rabbit stew."

Sammy asked, "But how can you stand eating those cute little animals?"

Mr. Hill said, "Son, I figure the garden will feed either them, or me. So I have to get rid of them."

Bill said, "Then we will help. You, too, Sammy?"

Sammy said, "Me, too."

Mr. Hill said, "Fine. I can use all the help I can get. Nine o'clock all right for you?"

Lord Frost said, "We will see you then!"

Sammy shouted, "Yipee! It's the big rabbit round-up!"

Bill said, "But how about what you said about the cute little rabbits?"

Sammy just stuck out his tongue.

Chapter 8: The Break-In on Clover Road

All afternoon the Woodlanders, the Hunters, and Lord and Lady Frost walked around the farm.

They got back to the farmhouse for

4:00 tea. The little sandwiches tasted good, but the Woodlanders were tired.

They were muddy.

But worst of all, they hadn't found anything.

Mrs. Tandy said, "Oh, well. We will find that old Roman place yet."

Mr. Hunter said, "We may have to start digging test holes."

Dave said, "At least we can be pretty sure the villa's on Wind-Born Farm. After the rabbit round-up tomorrow, we can keep looking."

They said good-bye to the Frosts and walked over to their cars.

Mrs. Hunter said, "At last you'll have a chance to look over your new house, Becky."

Mrs. Tandy said, "It's so beautiful, I love it already."

Soon the Woodlanders were back at

1010 Clover Road.

Mrs. Tandy opened the door while Sammy and Bill took Dave up the steps. Then they all went into the living room.

Mrs. Tandy gasped.

Sammy whispered, "HOLY CATS!"

The living room was a mess.

The drawers of the table and desk had been dumped out on the floor.

Most of the books were pulled out of the bookshelves.

The couch had been pushed forward

and the pillows pulled off.

They raced into the other rooms. Everything was torn up.

Dave called the police, who showed up right away, but didn't find any clues.

It took the Woodlanders two hours to get things back in place.

Mrs. Tandy said, "Well, at least I've had a chance to look over our new house from top to bottom."

Sammy said, "More like from bottom to top. Everything's all upside-down."

Kathy said, "Why would somebody do this? What could they want?"

Bill asked, "Should we call the Hunters and tell them what happened?"

Dave said, "We should. I'll call them."

Ben Hunter answered the phone. Dave told him what had happened.

Mr. Hunter said, "Oh, no. I'm so

sorry! And I'm SO glad Sammy gave the old silver box to me! What if we had left it in your house!"

Dave said, "The box! Could that be what they were looking for? But no one else knows about it."

Then Bill said, "Let me talk to him. Mr. Hunter, just in case someone IS after the box, I think you should keep it with you at all times. Even sleep with it."

Mr. Hunter said, "You're right. That thief could try anything. Be sure to lock all the doors and windows.

"I'll ask the police to check your house all night."

When Bill hung up the phone, Dave said, "I'll check the doors right now."

He wheeled to the back door and opened it to lock the screen door.

But he saw something.

It was a tiny piece of black cloth

caught on the screen-door spring!

Dave picked it up. He put it on his lap and locked both doors.

Then he went back to the other Woodlanders.

He said, "Come here, everyone. I think I found a clue. This torn piece of cloth was hooked on the screen door."

Sammy said, "Wow! Looks like the thief didn't take anything ... he LEFT something instead!"

Kathy said, "Well, let's keep our eyes open for someone with a torn black sleeve."

Mrs. Tandy said, "Well, you know, here's what I think. I think we have a bigger mystery on our hands than we thought.

"And I think Ben Hunter knows something about it."

Dave said, "Well, I sure hope he lets us in on it soon."

Chapter 9:
The Rabbit Round-Up

The next morning they met the Hunters for breakfast.

Roger was with them.

He said, "Good morning, young sirs

and miss. Good morning, Mrs. Tandy."

He lifted Bunny to his chair.

Sammy said, "Hey, that's a great blue coat you're wearing, with those shiny brass buttons. I like it a lot more than your black one."

All of a sudden Bill got a funny look on his face.

Dave and Kathy had the same funny look.

They were all thinking about the black scrap of cloth!

Why wasn't Roger wearing his black coat?

Could the sleeve be torn?

By 9:00 they were all with Lord and Lady Frost in the rabbit field.

Roger said, "I'll look after Bunny during the hunt. He and I will take a little walk. Then he won't be in the way."

James Hill walked up with a cage in

one hand and a big pile of nets on the other arm.

He said, "Good morning to you all! I'm so glad you could join me!"

Sammy pointed to the cage. He said, "What kind of animal is THAT?"

A skinny yellow rat-like thing, about as long as a ruler, raced around inside the cage.

Mr. Hill said, "It's my ferret. Don't get your fingers near him. He's as mean as a tiger, and fast. I couldn't catch rabbits without him."

Kathy said, "Look at his eyes! They're bright red!"

Mr. Hill said, "Here we go. First we get over to those bushes.

"See the holes below them everywhere? Lay the nets down to cover the holes, or put stones over them."

It took them quite a while.

Dave said, "Now what?"

Lord Frost said, "Rabbits make tunnels that all join together. The tunnels end up here at these holes."

Mr. Hill said, "And rabbits are afraid of ferrets."

He lowered the ferret into a hole.

They heard it running down. In a few seconds dozens of squealing rabbits began to run out of other holes, into nets.

Lord Frost said, “In a minute we can pick up the nets, rabbits and all. Then put them into the bags.”

Mrs. Tandy said, “But where is your mean little ferret?”

Mr. Hill said, “He should be up here, in one of the nets.”

They looked carefully into every net as they filled the bags.

Sammy said, “I hate this. These rabbits are so scared!”

Lady Frost said, “I do, too, my dear. But they have to go.”

They took the bags of rabbits down to the truck.

Mr. Hill brought three spades back with him. He said, “Looks like we will have to dig my ferret out.”

They took turns digging in the dirt

around the bushes. There were roots and rocks in it. It was hard work.

Every few minutes they found a tunnel and followed it, trying to dig out the ferret. They found tunnels everywhere, but not the ferret.

Roger and Bunny came back.

Bunny sat in the warm sun playing with stones. Everyone was getting hungry and hot.

Then Bunny walked over to Dave and put a flat stone in his lap.

"Pretty flower," Bunny said.

Dave said, "That's not a flower, Bunny, that's a stone."

Bunny climbed up on Dave's lap. He said, "No! See? Pretty. Pretty flower."

Dave picked up the stone to look at it.

He yelled, "HOLY SMOKE! Hey, everybody! Look what Bunny found!"

His voice sounded so strange they all

ran over to him.

Mr. Hunter reached out and took the stone. There was a bright flower painted on it.

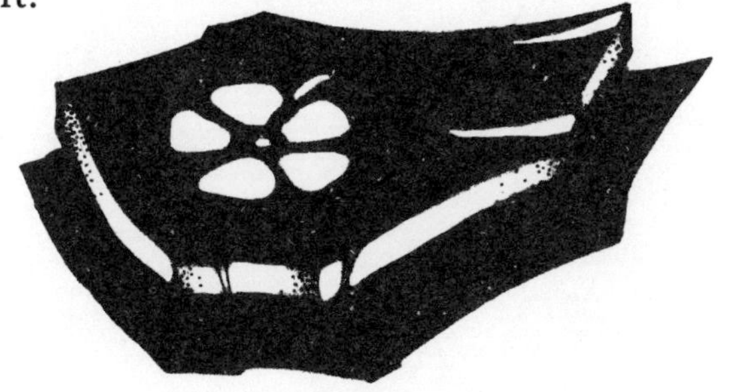

He said, "My word! This isn't a stone at all. This is a piece of wall tile. Old Roman wall tile."

Mr. Hunter's face turned red.

He picked Bunny up and held him high in the air. He hugged Dave until Dave could hardly breathe.

Mr. Hunter shouted, "THIS IS THE PLACE! WE FOUND IT! Here's where we dig! We are standing right above the old Roman villa!"

Chapter 10: The Real Roger

They all went back to the Frosts' farm to phone the national museum in London.

Mrs. Hunter said, "Why don't I start to phone the workers now?"

Lady Frost said, "Go up to the study and use that phone. It won't be so noisy there."

Then Mr. Hunter said, "We need to buy the tools for the dig. I'll make the list.

"And while I'm in town, I'll put the silver snuff box in the bank. It's locked in the trunk of the car now."

Roger said, "My word, sir. I hope it's all right. I'll go get it for you. Then I'll take Bunny for a walk while you get your list ready."

He turned to Mrs. Tandy. He said, "Perhaps you would care to take a turn around the small sheep field with us."

Sammy began to smile. He teased, "Her boyfriend back home, Chief Hemster, isn't going to like this!"

Mrs. Tandy laughed. "Then come along, Sammy, and be my guard."

They went outside.

But suddenly Roger raced back into the room. His long legs flew. He looked like a very upset stork.

He said, "Your trunk's been broken into! Someone pried it open. It looks like they used a crowbar!"

Mr. Hunter said, "And the silver box?"

Roger said, "I'm sorry to tell you, sir. It's gone."

Bill, Dave, and Kathy all looked at

each other, wondering the same thing about Roger.

Sammy ran in just as Mrs. Hunter came down the stairs.

He said, "My box! Jonathan Hunter's box! Your box! Someone stole it! It's gone! I just searched the whole car."

Mrs. Hunter said, "No it isn't, Sammy. I have it safe in my purse. I was worried when Ben left it in the trunk, so I went back for it. Here it is."

Mr. Hunter and Sammy both ran over to her and hugged her.

Kathy said, "Who in the world would be trying to break into the car?"

Dave said, "The same one who broke into Mrs. Tandy's house ... our house ... at Martin-on-the-River."

Mr. Hunter said, "All right, everyone. The time has come for me to fill you all in on what's going on."

Roger said, "Right, sir."

Mr. Hunter called Mrs. Tandy and Bunny inside.

They all sat in the big farm kitchen and listened to Ben Hunter.

He asked, "Have you ever heard of people being in the treasure-hunting business?"

Dave said, "Do you mean like the people who look for sunken ships, to find gold?"

Mr. Hunter said, "Exactly. Well, a man who owns such a business came to the museum this spring.

"He said a crooked treasure-hunting company was going to try to find and steal the Roman gold.

"He had been asked to join them. Instead he came to warn us."

Kathy asked, "How could they find it when the museum couldn't even find it?"

Mr. Hunter said, "Our museum couldn't risk spending all its money on finding a villa that might not exist.

"The crooks had a huge amount of money. They planned to buy some special equipment, and dig test holes this summer.

"When they found the spot, they were going to buy the land, or steal the treasure at night."

Bill asked, "What did the museum do?"

Mr. Hunter said, "First they decided to put all the money they could into the search for the villa this summer.

"Then they called Scotland Yard. That's England's detective force."

Dave asked, "What did Scotland Yard do?"

Mr. Hunter said, "Believe it or not, they told the museum to hire a butler.

"But not just ANY butler. A very tall, smart butler. Roger Smith, to be exact."

The Woodlanders and Lord and Lady Frost all stared at Roger.

Sammy said, "You're a detective?"

Bill said, "With Scotland Yard? And I was thinking you might be the thief!"

Lord Frost said, "Goodness! An undercover man, right here at Wind-Born."

Kathy said, "So you keep an eye on Bunny, and on everything else, too."

Mrs. Tandy said, "It must be very hard

for a person as tall as you to snoop around without people catching on."

Lady Frost said, "Not if everyone thinks he's really a butler!"

Roger said, "And I AM really a butler. Have been for seventeen years, in more than fifty cases. I carry no papers that show anything else."

Sammy said, "You mean no one knows that Roger the butler is really a super-hero?"

Roger made a deep bow. "Roger the butler at your service, ladies and gentlemen."

Chapter 11: Gold! Gold!

Early the next morning the rabbit field at Wind-Born was as busy as an anthill.

The Woodlanders, their friends, and more than fifty workers were chopping down hundreds of thorny bushes.

They made four huge piles of them to burn later.

Now all the rabbit holes could easily be seen.

Then the workers put up a large tent for shelter from the rain.

Next they pushed poles into the ground. They tied white strings to them. The field became a checkerboard of big squares. Mrs. Hunter gave each square a number.

Mr. Hunter said, "If the workers find anything, they'll call us over. We will draw what they find in the right square, and write down what it is."

Mrs. Hunter said, "Then the workers will use small shovels to dig it out very carefully.

"After they fill a basket with dirt, they'll sift it with a screen."

Sammy said, "You mean you'll even save the tiny pieces of things?"

Mr. Hunter said, "Yes. There may be a lot of broken pieces in one square of earth. We save them to glue together."

Already two diggers were waving to Mr. and Mrs. Hunter. They had found more tile chips!

Then everyone started digging. Even Lord and Lady Frost had shovels.

Dave, from his wheelchair, was digging, too.

Bunny had a shovel about as big as a spoon. He was covered with dirt after the first five minutes.

In about an hour Roger put down his spade. He walked over to the Woodlanders.

He said, "What do you say to a walk? We can stroll through the hills and the fruit trees around the rabbit field. Bunny isn't coming. He's too busy digging."

Dave said, "I'll stay here. I'm just getting the hang of it."

Kathy said, "I'll stay with you, Dave."

But Bill, Sammy, and Mrs. Tandy went off with Roger.

As they climbed up the first hill, they could see the rabbit field spread out below.

Mrs. Tandy said, "It's like a scene from a movie."

Roger said, "And it looks like we aren't the only ones who find it interesting. See those rabbit hunters?"

On the next hill over stood two men

with shotguns. They were looking down toward the dig. They had field glasses.

Roger led his group toward them. He said, "Jolly fine morning to hunt. I'm afraid we've spoiled the rabbit field with the dig. But these hills are full of rabbits."

Sammy kicked Bill. He whispered, "Hey, look! Those men are wearing shiny city shoes. Some hunters!"

Bill whispered back, "Hey, is that a torn spot on that man's sleeve?"

The hunters kept looking at the field.

One of them said in a mean voice, "Don't worry about us. We can find plenty to hunt."

Roger led the Woodlanders away. Then he did a strange thing. He turned and ran up the hill in back of the men.

He pulled a big white rag from his pocket. He waved it once in the air.

Then he stuffed it back into his pocket.

A minute later they heard shouting below them.

One of the diggers was waving her arm wildly. Her voice was REALLY LOUD! It rang out across the field and up the hillsides.

She shouted, "I found a gold coin! Come here, take a look! Gold! Gold!"

Mr. Hunter ran over. He took one

look. He wrapped the coin in white paper and put it into his pocket.

He shook the woman's hand and pounded her on the back.

Then he dropped to his hands and knees and grabbed a small shovel. He pushed some dirt around.

In a moment he was standing up and jumping up and down. He held another coin in his hand.

He shouted, "The treasure! It may be right below our feet!"

The workers at the dig all began to cheer and throw their hats in the air.

Mr. Hunter yelled, "We won't dig in this square anymore today. I'll have to arrange for guards and a truck for the gold. We can start digging it out tomorrow.

"Roger and I will camp here tonight." He wrapped the second coin in paper.

Everyone was so excited, it took quite a while for them to get back to digging in the other squares.

But at last the diggers were back at work.

Mr. Hunter waved Lord and Lady Frost into the tent. He called Bill to get the Woodlanders. Roger brought Bunny.

Roger set him down on the floor. He took a bunch of plastic animals out of his pocket. He said, "Here you are, Sir Bunny."

Then Mr. Hunter said, "I want to show you all something."

He took a box from his pocket.

It was the silver box from Heart Castle.

He opened it.

Inside lay the paper from Jonathan Hunter.

The two gold coins were gone!

Chapter 12: Setting the Trap

Mr. Hunter said, "Don't worry. Our coins weren't stolen. Here they are."

He took the two papers out of his pocket. He took the gold coins out of them.

Sammy said, "Wait a minute! Those are the coins you and that worker found!"

Bill said, "You mean you didn't find new coins? Hey! You hid our coins there at the dig, didn't you?"

Mr. Hunter nodded. "Yes. Then she and I acted as if we had found new ones."

Kathy said, "But why?"

Roger said, "Let me explain. Don't look so sad, Sammy. We will find all the gold someday.

"But it will take months. Or years. And every minute we looked for it, the treasure hunters would be there ... ready to attack."

Mr. Hunter said, "You see, we must dig everything so carefully. And we have to map it all because we want to save the Roman villa."

Dave said, "Isn't there any way to get rid of the treasure hunters?"

Roger said, "The only way would be to jail them."

He went on. "Here's the whole plan. Today Lord and Lady Frost had their lawyers give the rabbit field to the National Trust.

"It no longer belongs to any one person. It belongs to all of the country."

Mr. Hunter said, "Now it comes under national law. Right now we are putting up signs all over the rabbit field. Here's one."

Kathy read, "National Trust. Keep Out."

Roger said, "Also, we are putting a rope fence around it."

Sammy laughed. He said, "A rope fence won't keep out those crooks!

"They got into our new house.

"They got into Mr. Hunter's car trunk.

"They'll walk right through a rope fence and start to dig."

Dave said, "Wait a minute! That's the point, isn't it? You want them to walk right into the field!"

Kathy said, "I get it! The minute they do, Scotland Yard will grab them!"

Roger said, "Exactly right! A bunch of the workers here are from Scotland Yard.

"One of our people is the woman who pretended to find the coin.

"We chose her because she has a loud voice. We had to be sure she'd be heard by the spies on the hill."

Bill said, "Spies on the hill? Then we were right! Those guys with the fancy shoes weren't rabbit hunters!"

Kathy said, "And now the crooks think we are starting to dig out the gold tomorrow."

Dave said, "So they'll have to try to get it themselves tonight."

Roger said, "Right-o! The crooks will be expecting only Mr. Hunter and me to be on guard.

"The plan is to head for the tent as soon as it gets dark.

"They'll probably send some one to the tent to take us prisoner."

Mrs. Hunter said, "That sounds so dangerous, Ben."

Mr. Hunter said, "Roger and I will be very careful."

Roger said, "Besides, Mr. Hunter and I

will sneak back out of the tent. They'll only THINK we are there."

Sammy asked, "Can we help out tonight?"

Roger said, "We surely do need your help. There are ten Scotland Yard people in the digging crew.

"They will hide in the field tonight. When the treasure hunters cross the rope fence, our people will arrest them."

Dave asked, "What should WE do?"

Roger said, "Help us spot them as soon as they enter the rabbit field.

"There's a road coming in from Mr. Hill's farm, and one coming in from the Frosts' place.

"Lord and Lady Frost and the Hunters can watch the Frosts' road. The Woodlanders can watch Mr. Hill's road.

"I'll show you where to park so you'll be hidden, and give you some two-way radios to use."

Roger went on. "The minute one of you sees any sign of trouble, radio us."

Mrs. Tandy said, "Then Scotland Yard can make the arrest."

Sammy asked, "Why can't you just listen for their motor noise, and watch for their lights?"

Roger said, "Because they will be driving without lights.

"And they'll have the most quiet, modern trucks ever made.

"They are crazy to get that gold. We have to be sure they don't surprise us."

Kathy asked, "How will we know when you catch them?"

Roger said, "I'll radio you when we've made the arrests. Then you can enter the field.

"Right now we should all go back to our digging. Don't act strange in any way. Remember, we are all being watched through field glasses."

At last it was 5:00. Everyone left the dig except Roger and Mr. Hunter. The two men made a camp dinner outside near the tent.

Then they talked and yawned and nodded until 9:00.

It was dark, with only a sliver of moon.

Then they turned on a flashlight, and went into the tent.

They turned off the light.

All was quiet.

■ ■ ■

No one saw them sneak out of the tent a moment later.

No one saw Roger hide near a tree in the field.

No one saw Ben Hunter join his wife in their car.

Chapter 13: Grab Him!

A red rental car was hidden in some thick bushes.

Inside it the Woodlanders were slapping mosquitos and watching the road.

Sammy whispered, "I bet we've been slapping for half an hour already. I think I gave myself a black eye. I hit that last one awfully hard."

Bill said, "Just keep quiet and keep slapping."

Kathy said, "Do you hear anything?"

Mrs. Tandy answered, "Nothing so far. Maybe they're not coming on Mr. Hill's road at all!"

All of a sudden they heard Mr. Hunter's voice on their two-way radio.

"Two trucks coming on Frost Road. Just passing us now. One's carrying a tractor with a claw. We see twelve people all together, in and on the trucks."

Then Dave said, "I just saw a light shining on a moving car. Someone's coming on our road, too, with the lights turned off."

He grabbed the radio. He said, "Car coming on Hill Road. Can you hear me? Car on Hill Road!"

But he got no answer.

At that moment Scotland Yard's radios were turned off. The detectives were sneaking toward the treasure hunters' trucks to make the arrest.

Bill said, "Who would have thought those crooks would come from two different sides of the field?"

In the faint moonlight the Woodlanders saw the car drive past their hiding place.

It went into the roped-off part of the field, onto the hillside.

The car stopped right above the dig, near the tent.

Then, in the dark of night, two men got out. They began to sneak toward the tent.

Dave said, "What a mess! The thieves are in BACK of the Scotland Yard people. We've got to stop them."

Sammy was already out of the car, running after the men.

Bill was running right after him.

Dave called to Mrs. Tandy, "Switch the lights on! Drive right up into the field! Keep the car lights aimed at one of the crooks so he can't hide!

"And honk the horn!"

A Scotland Yard detective heard the noise.

He saw what was going on.

He ran up and grabbed the crook.

Mrs. Tandy drove on up the hillside to help Sammy and Bill.

Kathy and Mrs. Tandy jumped out and got Dave's wheelchair.

By then Sammy had dived at the other crook's legs and missed.

The crook ran a few steps more.

Sammy dived again and pushed him to his knees near a huge over-hanging rock.

The man grabbed a stone and was about to smash it down on Sammy's head.

Bill grabbed Sammy and pulled him to one side.

The crook swung the stone and fell. He rolled down the hillside into the arms of a detective.

But Bill and Sammy took a worse fall ... straight down ... just as Dave, Kathy, and Mrs. Tandy reached them.

The boys had rolled under the huge over-hanging rock. What looked like ground under the rock was only matted grass.

They fell right through it and dropped down about fifteen feet!

THUD! Sammy landed on his side. He was knocked out.

THUMP! Bill came down on his feet but fell forward onto his knees. He yelled, "HELP!"

They were in a deep, dark hole.

Roger came running.

He yelled to Kathy, "We've got the crooks! Where are Bill and Sammy?"

She said, "Right around this rock! Listen! I can hear Bill's voice coming from under this over-hanging part!"

Dave said, "There's a hole under it!"

By then, four detectives were gathered around the over-hang.

The Hunters and Lord and Lady Frost ran onto the hill side.

They all got on their stomachs and crawled forward around the hole. They shined their lights down. There were the boys.

Kathy called, "Sammy! Bill!"

Sammy slowly lifted his head and gave a sick smile. He said, "Where am I?"

Mr. Hunter yelled, "Great Scot! Look at those stone walls!"

Sammy said, "Are we in another tower? One that goes down instead of up?"

Bill said, "Wait a minute! Could this be a part of the villa?"

Mr. Hunter said, "You did it the hard way, lads, but you did it! You found the well of the old Roman villa!"

Sammy began to get up.

Roger called, "Don't do that, young sir. We will come down first to check you out. See if anything's broken. Stay lying down."

In a minute he and Ben Hunter went down a rope into the well.

By then the detectives had spotlights aimed into it.

Roger felt Sammy's arms and legs. He checked his ribs and head.

He said, "I think you're all right.

Move a bit. Let's see if it hurts."

Bill shouted, "He can't!"

Sammy laughed and said, "I'm not THAT hurt! I can move!"

Bill shouted, "But don't! Please!"

Slowly he pointed to the ground an inch in front of Sammy's nose.

Something lay shining in the dirt.

Bill asked, "Is that a gold coin? Don't move, Sammy, or it might get covered with dirt."

Mr. Hunter dropped onto his hands and knees. Slowly he reached over to the small coin. He lifted it out of the dirt.

He grabbed Bill in his usual bear hug.

He cried, "THE WELL! That's it! The Romans hid the gold in this well! This must be where Jonathan Hunter found the other two coins a hundred years ago!"

Later, back at the new house at Martin-on-the-River, everyone sat around the kitchen table. It was midnight.

Bunny was there, too. He and the Hunters, Lord and Lady Frost, Roger, two of the Scotland Yard detectives, and the Woodlanders, were eating oatmeal cookies with milk.

Mrs. Tandy and Dave were just putting a third batch of cookies into the oven.

Bill was saying, "I can't wait to start clearing that well tomorrow."

Mrs. Hunter said, "Those men will spend years in jail. We will have the gold safe long before they're out."

Bill said, "All those years ago young Jonathan Hunter must have found that well opening.

"He must have climbed down into it using the cracks between the stones as footholds. What a great detective he was."

Sammy said, "I never met him, but I'll never forget him."

Mr. Hunter said, "We can lower a ladder into the well tomorrow."

Kathy asked, "How many can work in it at once?"

Mr. Hunter said, "Four, I think, or five."

Sammy said, "It sure is lucky two of your detectives know about working at a dig."

Roger laughed. "And Bunny loves to dig, too. We thirteen will bring up those gold coins in short order."

"THIRTEEN!" yelled Sammy. "Not thirteen AGAIN. Thirteen's bad luck ... it ... well, wait a minute!"

He sat thinking.

Then he said, "All the thirteens I was afraid of at the beginning of the trip ... thirteen suitcases ... Flight one-thirteen ... Friday the thirteenth ... I think they all brought us GOOD luck!"

He went on. "Really good luck ... Heart Castle ... the silver box ... the Roman villa ... the gold in the well."

Sammy stood up. He reached across the table and counted out six cookies.

He laid them in a row in front of him and began to munch on one.

Grinning, he said, "I'm only eating these for you, guys. To bring good luck to the dig.

"See, I've had seven cookies. Six more

will make thirteen."

The others groaned. Then, laughing and munching, the Woodlanders and their friends talked about the Roman gold they would find tomorrow.